The DONUT CHEF

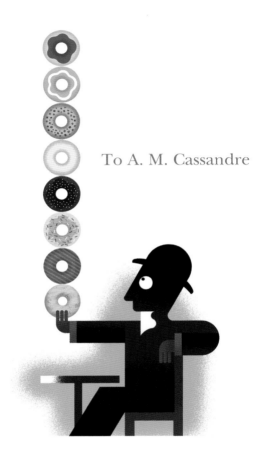

To A. M. Cassandre

Copyright © 2008 by Bob Staake.
All rights reserved. Published in the United States by Dragonfly Books, an imprint of Random House Children's
Books, a division of Random House, Inc., New York. Originally published in hardcover in the United States by
Golden Books, an imprint of Random House Children's Books, New York, in 2008.
Dragonfly Books with the colophon is a registered trademark of Random House, Inc.
Visit us on the Web! randomhouse.com/kids
Educators and librarians, for a variety of teaching tools, visit us at RHTeachersLibrarians.com
Library of Congress Control Number: 2007938198
ISBN 978-0-375-84403-4 (trade) — ISBN 978-0-375-94716-2 (lib. bdg.) — ISBN 978-0-385-36992-3 (pbk.)
MANUFACTURED IN CHINA
10 9 8 7 6
First Dragonfly Books Edition 2013

The DONUT CHEF

Donut Land

by Bob Staake

DRAGONFLY BOOKS · NEW YORK

Once upon a summer's day
A donut chef was heard to say:
"On this street where people stop,
I'll open up my donut shop!"
The store was cozy, made of brick.
He got it ready super-quick!
He washed the walls, he swept the floors,
He hung a sign above the doors!

He stacked his pots, he cleaned his pans,
He dusted off the ceiling fans.
He grabbed a spoon, then turned a knob,
And set the stove to do its job!

That donut chef, he worked so hard
By mixing flour, sugar, lard.
He baked his donuts fresh at dawn,
Then hoped by noon they'd all be gone!

At first one man walked in the store . . .

But then a line snaked out the door!
The donuts soon were all the rage—
Adored by folks of every age!

Soon word got out of this success—
And to another chef, no less,
Who said to him, "Your shop is through . . .
When *my* store opens next to you!"

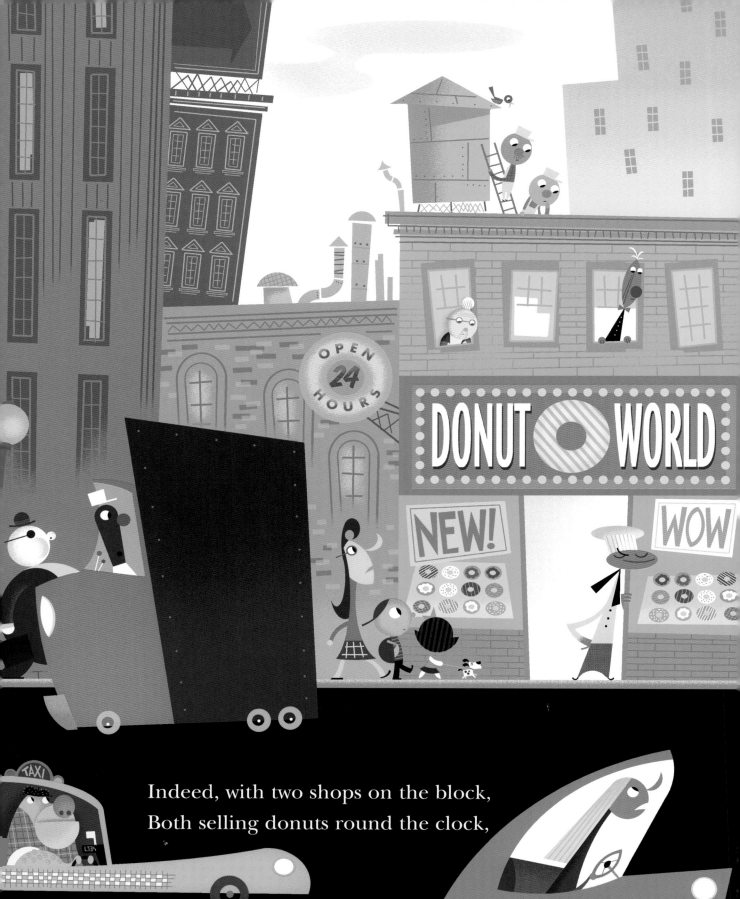

Indeed, with two shops on the block,
Both selling donuts round the clock,

Well, people asked—you might have guessed—
"Whose donuts are the very best?"

Two donut shops on one small street!
For customers they did compete!
Each used his donut-selling tricks
Before he closed his doors at six!

If one chef dropped his donut cost,
The next would add more chocolate frost!
If one would scream, "Buy two, get three!"
The other yelled, "But mine are FREE!"

They made new flavors, quite bizarre,
Like Cherry-Frosted Lemon Bar,
And Peanut-Brickle Buttermilk,
And Gooey Cocoa-Mocha Silk!

They tried new shapes beyond just rings—
Their donuts were such crazy things!
Some were square and some were starry,
Some looked just like calamari!
Some were airy, some were cone-y!
Some resembled macaroni!

It wasn't long before the sweets
Looked not at all like donut treats.
They'd lost their taste. They'd lost their soul.
They'd even lost their donut hole!

The chefs continued with their feud,
Cooked up more crazy frosted food.

Then in walked little Debbie Sue,
A teeny girl, just barely two.
She looked at all the donuts weird,
The flavors strange, the toppings smeared.
She looked and looked but could not find
The one that was her favorite kind.

"'Scuse me, Mister," said the tyke,
"But where's the donut that *I* like?
It isn't here, it isn't there—
You think it's under that éclair?"

"Oh, surely," said the chef with grace,
"*Your* donut's in this donut case!

"We've donuts laced with kiwi jam,
And served inside an open clam!
Donuts made with huckleberry
(Don't be scared; they're kind of hairy),
And donuts made from spiced rum pears,
So popular with millionaires!
We've donuts lighter than a wisp,
Donuts gooey, donuts crisp!
Donuts dressed just like a Shriner,
Donuts major! Donuts minor!
If we don't have it, you can bet
It can't be found—at least, not yet."

The choice of donuts left her dazed.
Said Debbie Sue, "But I want . . . *glazed!*"

"No one orders donuts glazed!"
The chef was startled, then amazed.
"A donut glazed? That's so old-time,
From when a donut cost a dime!"

"Hey, I like glazed!" a voice chimed in.
"Me too! I LOVE 'em! Where've they been?"
Then all the people sang in praise
Of simple donuts dipped in glaze!

The clever chef then got a thought,
And turned his stove to super-hot.

Flour, sugar (just a cup),
And in a bowl he mixed it up!

He let it cook, knew what to do,
And—*ding!*—the timer chimed on cue!

"Your donut's ready, Debbie Sue!"

She popped the donut in the air,
And in her mouth it landed there.
She chewed it, smiled, and gave a wink . . .

"Mmmmmmm! There's nothing quite like glazed, I think!"

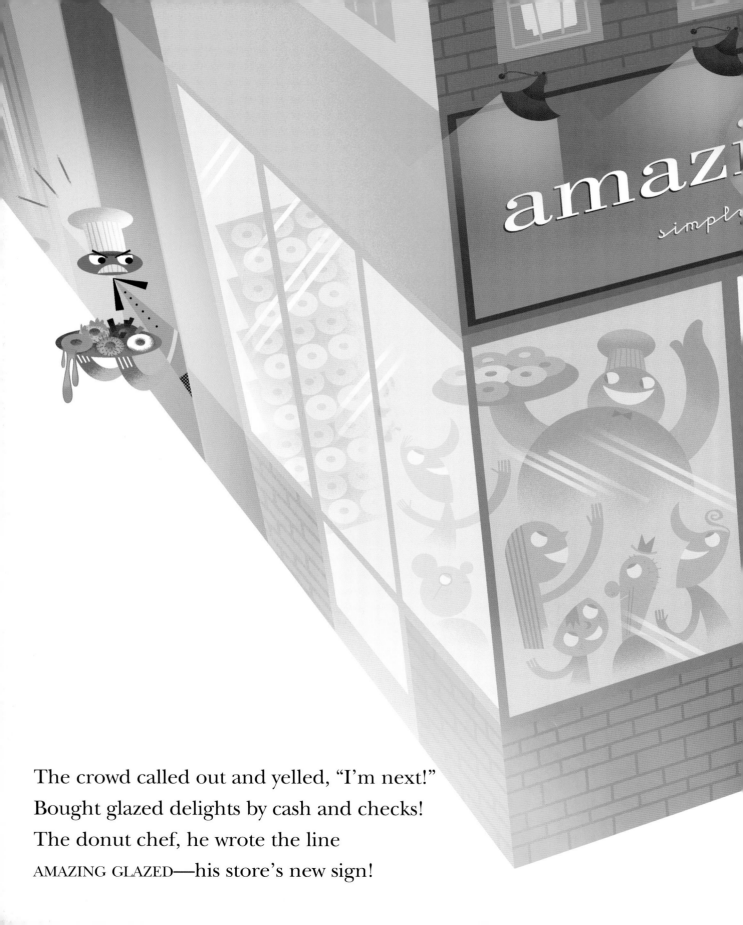

The crowd called out and yelled, "I'm next!"
Bought glazed delights by cash and checks!
The donut chef, he wrote the line
AMAZING GLAZED—his store's new sign!

Now throngs of people
  happily wait
To buy his donuts
  by the crate.
The donut chef,
  he'd never guessed,
Of all the flavors he did test,

That most folks love a glazed the BEST!